HAVE
A GO

Titles in the series:

Badger Publishing Limited, Oldmedow Road, Hardwick Industrial Estate, King's Lynn PE30 4JJ

Telephone: 01438 791037

www.badgerlearning.co.uk

HAVE A GO

A GO

JON MAYHEW

Have a Go ISBN 978-1-78837-199-5

Text © Jon Mayhew 2017
Complete work © Badger Publishing Limited 2017

Publisher: Susan Ross
Senior Editor: Danny Pearson
Editorial Coordinator: Claire Morgan
Copyeditor: Cheryl Lanyon
Designer: Bigtop Design Ltd
Cover: © Everett Collection Inc / Alamy Stock Photo

4 6 8 10 9 7 5

CHAPTER 1
OPEN ALL HOURS

Jamie Garson ducked under the fist swinging towards him and gave a quick jab to his attacker's stomach. His dad doubled up, pretending to be in agony. "Oof! You got me son!" he said, clutching his round tummy. "You could be the next James Bond."

"With muscles like mine?" Jamie laughed. "Not likely!"

"Give over, son," Dad said. "I bet you're a wow with all the girls at school. I know I used to be. Terry 'the Lad' Garson, that was me." He winked at Jamie.

"Dad!" Jamie mumbled. "You're so embarrassing sometimes!" He grinned, though. What a great evening. A film followed by a sneaky drink in Dad's local. Just Jamie and Dad.

Dad's phone buzzed and he pulled it out of his pocket. "Uh-oh," he said, winking at Jamie, "it's your mother." He read the message:

Can you bring some milk home?

"Looks like we've got a mission."

"Where are we going to find milk at this time?" Jamie said, pulling his jacket tight round his neck. "It's gone ten o'clock." It was a cold November night and anyone with any sense was indoors keeping warm.

"There's the corner shop," Dad said. "Mr Bajek's open all hours. We'd better be quick, though." They hurried along the road. Jamie looked at the houses where warm lights glowed behind drawn curtains. He wished he was home.

The corner shop was one of those places that stayed open all the time and sold everything, from milk and bread to birthday cards and little plastic toys. Dad pushed the door open and froze. Two men wearing ski masks and holding baseball bats stood in front of the shop counter. Mr Bajek clutched a fistful of banknotes, just about to hand it over.

"Oi!" Dad shouted.

One man ran away, barging past Dad and knocking Jamie against the door. The other swung his bat at Dad's head. Jamie's heart pounded and he yelled at his dad to duck. The bat hummed inches from Dad's face. Without thinking, Dad snatched a tin of baked beans from the counter and brought it down hard on the robber's head. He crumpled to the ground, out cold.

Dad stood there panting for a moment. Then Jamie ran forwards. "Dad, are you OK?" he asked. Dad nodded.

"Thank you, thank you!" Mr Bajek said, hurrying from behind the counter. Jamie could see ten- and twenty-pound notes scattered all over the newspapers laid out on the counter top. "You saved my shop. We must call the police and the ambulance."

Twenty minutes later, paramedics wheeled the robber into the back of an ambulance and a police officer climbed in after him. Some people took pictures and a police officer made notes as the shopkeeper told his story.

An officer called PC Lloyd took Jamie into the back of his car and Jamie explained what had happened. "He's a brave fella, your dad," PC Lloyd said. Jamie felt his cheeks going red and he couldn't stop the grin on his face. "We'll get all the details down and have you home in no time."

Mum looked like a ghost when she saw Jamie and Dad climbing out of the back of a police car. She came sprinting out of the front door in her dressing gown. "Terry! Jamie! What's happened?"

PC Lloyd held up a hand as if he was stopping traffic. "Don't worry, Mrs Garson, Jamie and your husband have had a bit of an adventure, that's all," he said.

"Adventure?" Mum said. "Oh, Terry, what have you done?"

The police officer grinned. "He stopped a robbery, Mrs Garson. Your husband is a bit of a hero, or he will be in the morning."

"A hero?" Mum muttered, glaring at Dad. "You were only meant to be getting some milk." She ran her fingers through Jamie's hair. "You had Jamie with you! What if he'd been hurt?"

"Mum, I'm fine, stop fussing," said Jamie.

PC Lloyd drove off and left Mum, Dad and Jamie sitting in the lounge, trying to calm down after all the excitement.

"I didn't go looking for trouble, love," Dad said.

Mum's eyes looked like they were going to pop out of her head. "But what if you get done for assault or something?" she said.

"Don't be daft," Jamie scoffed. "The fella in the shop had a ski mask on and a baseball bat. Dad just hit him with a tin of beans."

"Yeah, but I read in the paper about this bloke who fought off a burglar in his own home and still went to jail," said Mum. "The burglar sued him for compensation and everything."

"That's just stupid," Jamie muttered. "I bet it didn't really happen like that."

"It'll be fine," Dad said, puffing out his chest. "I bet you always fancied being married to a superhero!"

Mum rolled her eyes but Jamie saw a smile twitch in the corner of her mouth. She narrowed her eyes at Jamie. "Anyway, young man, you'll be like a zombie for school in the morning if you don't get to bed."

Jamie groaned. The moment of excitement had passed but Jamie felt wide awake. "I'm not tired, Mum," he said, but she packed him off. At least he'd have a tale to tell his friends tomorrow.

CHAPTER 2
FAME

Mum and Dad forgot to put the alarm clock on and Jamie's phone was out of charge. So the first thing that woke him up was the doorbell ringing. Jamie groaned and rolled over in bed. He heard someone going downstairs and opening the door, a murmured conversation and someone running back upstairs. "Terry! Terry!" Mum said as she ran past Jamie's bedroom door. "It's a man from the newspaper, he wants to interview you about last night!"

The news reporter looked up and smiled as Jamie shuffled down in his tracksuit bottoms and vest.

"Ah, are you Jamie?" he asked. "You must be very proud of your dad." The news reporter was in his twenties, with black hair and a trendy beard. He wore suit trousers and a shirt underneath a heavy, hooded parka coat. Jamie glanced at the bag with cameras and notepaper that sat on the sofa next to the news reporter.

"Yeah," Jamie said. "It was really scary."

The news reporter pulled out his notepad.
"You were there," he continued, "so, tell me what happened."

Jamie shrugged and told the man what he remembered. He wasn't sure if some of the things he remembered were bits of a film he'd seen. In his head, dad had struggled with the robber for ages, ducking punches and diving out of the way. "In the end, the robber had Dad by the throat and Dad just managed to grab the tin of beans and smack him in the head with it."

"Brilliant," the news reporter said, scribbling furiously. "It must have been terrifying for you."

"Yeah," Jamie agreed.

Mum came back into the room, dressed and with a mug of coffee for the news reporter. "Anyway, Jamie, you need to get to school. It's nearly ten. I'll write you a letter, explaining why you're late."

"Aw, Mum, do I have to?" Jamie asked. Jamie had to.

School was dull after all the excitement of the night before. Isaac, Faisal and Sam sat in the school canteen, listening in amazement as Jamie told his tale.

"Woah," Faisal said, before taking a huge bite out of his wrap, "the guy had a gun? And your dad went for him anyway? Respect!"

Jamie reddened. Had he mentioned a gun? Anyway, it didn't matter, the robber was armed.

"Yeah, Dad threw him over his shoulder, but it was a close thing."

Isaac looked surprised. "I didn't know your dad was such a good fighter," he said. "My dad wouldn't do that."

The rest of the afternoon dragged on. Jamie couldn't wait to get home. When the final bell rang, he sprinted towards the main door. Kids jostled and elbowed each other out of the way, yelling and laughing as they poured into the road outside. Teachers stood watching the students streaming out. Someone crashed into Jamie, sending them both stumbling into the wall.

"Watch where you're going, idiot!" Jamie snapped at the little Year seven boy with spiky blonde hair and big blue eyes; he looked like a three-year-old about to burst into tears.

Calder Fullwood stood behind him, towering over both of them. "You tell 'im, Garson, the kid's a pain. Always gettin' in my way," he said, giving the lad a kick as he stepped over him. Jamie dropped his gaze to the ground as Fullwood swept past him. The little lad scrambled to his feet and scurried between the other pupils like a frightened mouse. Jamie tried to tell him that his bag was open and half his books were hanging out, but the boy had gone. With a shrug Jamie followed him, picking up the dropped books as he went. The boy's name was David Robbins. Jamie collected the books together and dropped them at the office before hurrying home. *One good deed for the day,* he thought. *Maybe being a hero runs in the family.* He didn't see the black car sitting outside school or the men inside, watching him as he hurried home.

CHAPTER 3
HIT LIST

Jamie came home to find the kitchen table covered with newspapers. Each paper had a picture of Dad inside. He was doing various things in the photographs, such as standing next to Mum in the garden, holding a tin of beans in the kitchen, standing next to Mum AND holding a tin of beans. The headlines said things like: "Full of Beans Hero" or "Have-a-Go Hero Gives it Beans," or "Beanz Meanz Prizon," which Jamie didn't understand until Mum explained that it was based on an old advertisement for tinned beans.

Dad was full of himself. "I'm going on the telly tomorrow and a radio phone-in, too."

"On TV, Dad!" Jamie exclaimed. "Can I come too?"

Dad shrugged. "Sorry, son, they only asked for me. Anyway, I might not be on. They said they might not fit me in."

As it was, Dad got a full five minutes on Breakfast TV. Jamie watched it with Mum before he went to school. Dad sat holding a tin of beans, and explained how he'd hit the robber. "I don't think I did anything special," he said. "I'm sure anyone else would have done the same in my position."

They had a police officer and someone who talked about how more shops were being robbed and how dangerous opening late at night was these days.

By the time Jamie got to school, he had a little gang of followers from all year groups asking him questions and saying how brave his dad was. "Does your dad do Kung Fu or something?" one kid asked.

"Is he a police officer?"

"He's like a superhero or something," someone else said. "I wish my dad was a hero. He just sits at home, picking his nose and grumbling at the TV."

Jamie grinned. It was quite cool having a hero for a dad. It didn't stop when they got into school, either. Jamie's form tutor nodded to him and said, "Was that your dad on the TV this morning? You must be very proud."

By break time, Jamie couldn't believe the number of people who had spoken to him about his dad. He sat on one of the benches in the school yard with Isaac, Faisal and Sam, sharing a bag of crisps that someone had passed to Jamie. After two free bags, Jamie was full. "You'll have to get your dad to do this more often," Isaac said, grinning. "I could get used to free crisps and stuff!"

Jamie laughed. "Yeah, I called in at the corner shop on the way home last night and got a load of freebies," he said. "It's brilliant!"

"Get off me!" a voice yelled nearby. Jamie frowned and saw Calder Fullwood dragging David along by his school bag. The straps clung to David's elbows, pinning his arms to his side. He fell over backwards.

"He's always picking on that little kid," Isaac muttered. David scrambled to his feet and ran straight towards Jamie and Isaac. Without thinking, Jamie jumped to his feet as David ran past him. Fullwood loped along after him and tripped over Jamie's foot, sprawling on the ground face down.

David gave one fearful backwards glance and vanished into the crowds that filled the yard at break time. Fullwood scrambled to his feet. A slight graze marked his chin and his blazer and knees were mucky but he looked unharmed otherwise. He glared at Jamie. "What d'you do that for, Garson?" he said, pushing Jamie hard in the chest.

Jamie staggered back, almost sitting down again. His throat felt dry. Jamie wasn't a fighter by any stretch of the imagination. *Neither was Dad*, he thought. *He wouldn't have let someone like Fullwood push him round when he was at school.* "Just pick on someone your own size, Fullwood," Jamie said, trying to push him back. Calder Fullwood stood a full head taller than Jamie. His shoulders felt strong and he didn't move an inch when Jamie pushed him.

"Oh yeah? You goin' to make me, Garson? Big hero like your pathetic dad, are you?" Fullwood snarled and, without warning, his fist swung from nowhere.

Stars exploded before Jamie's eyes and his neck and jaw went numb. It felt to Jamie like someone had grabbed the side of his head and twisted it round, then pushed him down onto the bench. Pain rushed across his face and he tasted blood in his mouth. Tears stung the backs of his eyes as he tried to work out what had happened. He sat doubled up on the bench. Another stab of pain lanced through the side of his head and he realized that Fullwood had hit him again. This time, his head went down and clipped the armrest of the wooden bench, sending another wave of pain through his forehead.

"Just remember what happens to heroes, Garson," Fullwood snarled in his ear. "They get a good kickin'. Just like your dad will as soon as we catch up with him."

Fullwood stalked off, leaving Jamie sitting dazed on the bench. Kids crowded round him. "Are you going to get him, Jamie?"

"Should I tell Mr Bennett?" someone else asked.

"Does he need the first aid room?"

Isaac grabbed Jamie by the shoulder and pushed him towards the toilets. Faces swam past Jamie, voices echoed in his throbbing head. He knew he was crying. His neck and lip pulsed and he just wanted to run home. "Come on, mate," Isaac said.

It was cool in the toilets and Isaac got Jamie to splash some cold water on his face. Jamie felt sick boiling up from his stomach and he stuck his head over the toilet. The door banged open and David came storming in, tears racing down his cheeks.

"You OK?" Jamie croaked.

"No!" David snapped. "Fullwood has just thrown all my books in the waste food skip at the back of the kitchen and he's going to get me after school. Thanks a lot. *Hero!*" He turned and slammed the door as he left the toilets.

Jamie looked at Isaac and shrugged. "Can't win them all, eh?" he said, trying to smile but it hurt too much.

"Never mind him, Jamie," Isaac said. "What about Fullwood? What was all that about your dad getting beaten up?"

Jamie winced and touched his swollen lip. "I don't know," he said. "But what can Fullwood do to my dad? He's just a kid like you and me."

Isaac shrugged. "I don't know either, Jamie, but you'd better watch out for Fullwood. You're on his 'hit list' now."

CHAPTER 4
YOUR BROTHER

Isaac, Faisal and Sam tried to get Jamie to report the attack by Fullwood. "You've got to," Faisal said. "He's been throwing his weight around for too long now. Someone has to tell."

"I'll just end up getting in trouble for fighting," said Jamie. "What will Dad think if I let the teachers solve all my problems?"

"He won't think anything," Sam said. "He'll think you did the right thing, maybe."

"What would you know about what my dad thinks?" Jamie snapped. "He wouldn't have run crying to the teachers at the first sign of trouble."

Sam looked hurt. "Suit yourself," he said.

"Yeah, I will," Jamie muttered and stormed off to his next lesson. Calder Fullwood met him around the next corner, slamming him against the wall.

"Some hero you are," Fullwood said, pushing his face into Jamie's. "You're just a fake. What are you?"

Jamie bit his lip but Fullwood slammed him against the wall again. The pain in his head and neck came back stronger. "I'm a fake," Jamie muttered, feeling the tears sting his eyes again.

"Yeah, and when my brother gets out on bail, he's goin' to come lookin' for your dad," Fullwood said. "Then we'll see how much of a hero he is, too."

Jamie stared at Fullwood. "Your brother?" he said, frowning. "The robber in the shop was your brother?"

"Too right he was," Fullwood said, pushing Jamie back again. He stepped away, releasing Jamie. "Just you wait." He stalked off.

Dad wasn't home when Jamie got back from school. Mum's eyes widened when she saw his fat lip and bruised head. "What happened to you?" she asked.

"Just a rugby accident," he lied. "I banged heads in a tackle, that's all. I'm fine. Stop fussing. Where's Dad?"

Mum rolled her eyes. "He's gone down to London," she said, trying to dab Jamie's face with a damp cloth. "Another TV interview. Why they can't do them at a studio nearer home, I don't know. And so last-minute, too."

A stab of anger surged through Jamie. While Dad was showing off on TV, Jamie was getting the crap kicked out of him. *Why can't he be here?* he thought. *I could warn him, then.*

School didn't get any better the next day. His dad's celebrity had worn off almost overnight and Fullwood seemed to be waiting for Jamie around every corner. "What's this?" Fullwood said, dragging Jamie's books out of his bag. "Ooh, the boy hero does his homework, eh? Sets a good example to us all." Fullwood selected the history exercise book from the pile he'd pulled from the bag and tore it in half. "There you go, Garson, hand that one in." He turned to Faisal and Sam who stood watching. "I'd better not see you two hanging around with this loser again or I might decide you want some of the same treatment."

The two lads backed away.

Jamie walked home alone that night after school. He thrust his hands deep in his pockets. It was late because of the history detention he'd been given. "Sorry, Jamie," the history teacher had said, "but if you forget your book, you get kept in. That's the rule." Of course, Jamie hadn't forgotten his book, the two halves lay at the bottom of his bag. When he got home, he was going to have to copy up everything into a new exercise book that evening.

The noise of a car engine snapped Jamie out of his thoughts and he turned around. An old, black Volkswagen roared along the road and then bounced up onto the pavement right by him. Jamie's heart thumped, he leaped back, falling over a litter bin. The car engine growled and Jamie felt the draft of air as its wheels skimmed inches from him then skidded back onto the road. As the car vanished in a cloud of blue smoke, Jamie caught sight of Fullwood laughing at him from the rear window.

Jamie limped home to find Dad sitting on the sofa, slurping a cup of tea and chatting down the phone. He gave Jamie a nod and carried on talking. "Of course I can come, yeah, it would be an honour," he said and then laughed. "Well, it's nice to be an inspiration…"

"You all right, Jamie?" Mum said, frowning at him. "You look a bit pale…"

"Yeah, I'm fine," he said, "just got loads of homework, that's all."

Dad came into the kitchen and clapped his hands together. "That was St Mary's Prep School, wanting me to speak at their prize-giving evening about public responsibility…"

"What would you know about responsibility?" Jamie snapped and stormed out of the kitchen. He ran upstairs and slammed his bedroom door behind him. Lying on his bed, he listened to Mum and Dad arguing about him in the kitchen. In the end, he heard Dad's heavy tread coming up the stairs.

"Are you OK, son?" asked Dad.

"Yeah, fine," Jamie replied, turning the pages of a textbook but not really looking at them.

"Then what was all that about downstairs?" Dad asked.

Jamie shrugged but didn't look up. "Dunno."

"I thought you'd be happy about me being on the TV and radio and stuff."

"I am," Jamie said. "It's just… well, what happens when that robber gets out of prison?"

Dad shrugged this time. "What d'you mean?"

"I mean, what if he wants to get even or something?"

Dad snorted. "He'd better not come near here," he said. "I've stocked up on tinned food." Jamie could tell Dad was joking but he could hear nervousness in his voice.

The sound of a revving engine interrupted their conversation and Jamie went to look out of his bedroom window. A black Volkswagen sat on the other side of the road from Jamie's house. *Fullwood!* Jamie thought.

"That's a bit of a racket," Dad mumbled. "Who's making all that noise?" He came over to the window just as the driver did a wheel spin and screeched off up the road in a cloud of blue smoke. "Idiot. He'll ruin his tyres doing that."

Dad shrugged and went downstairs, leaving Jamie staring down the street. Fullwood knew where they lived.

CHAPTER 5
ALONE

Breakfast was quiet. Dad had caught an early train somewhere to do another interview. "It's just his fifteen minutes of fame, Jamie, don't worry, it'll pass," Mum said, checking her purse before heading off for work.

"Fifteen minutes of fame?" Jamie said with his mouth full of cornflakes.

"Yeah. Apparently, someone once said that in the future everyone would be famous for fifteen minutes. Well, it's your dad's turn. He'll be back tomorrow."

Jamie checked up and down the street anxiously the next morning but there was no sign of Fullwood or his friends in the car. He walked down the street to the corner shop where Sam and Faisal usually met him, but they weren't there.

As he walked, Jamie became aware of the car rolling slowly alongside him in the road. He tried to pretend he hadn't noticed but the driver kept revving the engine. Jamie glanced over at the black Volkswagen just as Fullwood leaned out of the window and poked two fingers at him, imitating a gun. "Brrap!" Fullwood shouted and then the car sped off, the tyres squealing again and making Jamie's heart thump. He walked on, increasing his pace. Soon he was jogging, desperate to get to school before Fullwood came around again in the car. But what was safe about school? Fullwood would be there and what would he do this time? Punch him again? Wreck another book? It sounded stupid, but Fullwood knew what he was doing. These were Jamie's GCSE years; if he lost a book, he couldn't revise.

At school, he saw Isaac standing by the lockers. He glanced over at Jamie who raised a hand to wave but Isaac walked off as if he hadn't noticed him. Jamie stared round the corridor and saw a smirking Fullwood leaning against the door with his arms folded.

The days began to blur for Jamie. Travelling to and from school was scary. He never knew if Fullwood and his mates with the car would appear. He started to vary his route home, ducking down alleyways and running across the park to avoid them. Nobody walked with him any more, everyone was too scared. He wandered around school in a daze, not really listening to lessons. Isaac, Sam and Faisal seemed too frightened to talk to him. "Fullwood's a full-on psycho," Faisal said to him in the dinner queue, one day. "He nearly broke Sam's arm when he thought Sam had been talking to you. He's got Isaac's mobile number and keeps texting threats to him." He glanced around. "Look, I've got to go. I just wish your dad had never tackled that guy in the shop, that's all."

"You and me both," Jamie muttered as he watched Faisal hurry away through the crowded dinner hall.

Two weeks had passed since the attempted robbery and Dad seemed to be getting more than his fifteen minutes of fame. Jamie had stopped watching his television appearances but he had to admit that Dad could talk quite well on TV. He didn't 'um' or 'ah' on screen at all and he even managed to get the odd corny joke in too, usually about beans making you fart. Jamie didn't see the funny side any more.

One night, he lay awake in bed and stared at the ceiling. His mind wouldn't switch off and kept swirling all his thoughts around like a big tumble-dryer. Over and over it would go, thinking about everything. Then he heard the car engine. He recognized it immediately and closed his eyes, breathing deeply to stop his heart from thumping out of his chest. The anxiety rose in his throat. *Stop being stupid*, he thought, slamming his fist down on the mattress. *He can't harm you, you're in your house.* His breathing became faster and he felt sweat trickle down his back. He curled up into a ball. *Just go away!*

A car door slammed and Jamie heard the sound of breaking glass then a muffled 'Whumf!' An orange flash illuminated his room for a second. He ran over to the window. The red lights of the car vanished up the street, but flames licked up Jamie's front door. They'd set fire to the house!

CHAPTER 6
COME LOOKIN'

Jamie leaped up and barged into Mum and Dad's room. Dad was away but Mum woke suddenly. "Jamie! What is it?" she mumbled, still groggy.

"Fire," Jamie yelled. "We have to get out the back door."

Smoke filled the hall as they coughed and spluttered their way to the bottom of the stairs. Jamie could see the orange flames leaping up the outer part of the front door. The glass had cracked and the house stank of melted plastic and paint.

Mum's mobile lay on the kitchen table and she snatched it up as they hurried out into the back garden. Jamie coughed and gagged as he sucked in the fresh, cold night air. Somewhere a siren wailed but Jamie could hear something else, a car engine disappearing into the distance. He knew exactly who had done this.

"So, you've no idea who might have done this?" PC Lloyd said to Jamie as they sat in the kitchen, sipping tea. The fire brigade had responded fast and put the fire out. Mum sat turning her mug around in her fingers, sniffling up the tears. Jamie just felt numb.

"No," he said. The house smelled of smoke but the fire hadn't done much more than melt the front door a bit.

"Well, I don't want to alarm you, but do you think it could be connected with your father's heroics the other week?" PC Lloyd said. "Have you had any threats at all? Unpleasant phone calls or letters? Anything like that?"

Mum shook her head. "No," she said. "Just TV, newspaper and radio people phoning for Terry all the time."

PC Lloyd nodded and stared at Jamie. "Yeah, he's become a bit of a local celebrity, hasn't he?" he said.

"Do you think someone could be jealous or something?" Mum said.

"I don't know," said PC Lloyd. "That petrol bomb was dangerous. It could have burned the whole house down. What school do you go to, Jamie?"

The question came so out of the blue that Jamie didn't have time to even think. "Hinderton Academy," he said. "The one just up the road."

"Do you know Calder Fullwood?" PC Lloyd asked, raising his eyebrows.

Jamie could feel his cheeks reddening. "No," he said. "Well, yeah. Everyone knows Fullwood, he's a pyscho."

"Jamie!" Mum said, putting her cup down.

PC Lloyd gave a grim smile. "It's OK, Mrs Garson," he said. "I've heard Calder Fullwood described in much more unflattering terms. But he hasn't threatened you in any way, Jamie?"

Jamie thought his face must look like a tomato about to explode by now. "No," he said. "Why would he do that?"

"No reason," PC Lloyd said. "It was his brother that your dad clobbered with the tin of beans, that's all."

Jamie looked at his hands and picked at his fingernails. *Tell him, tell him, tell him,* he thought. *It'll all be over then and you can go back to being friends with Faisal, Sam and Isaac. Tell him, now.* But Jamie shrugged. "No," he said, flatly. "He hasn't been near me."

PC Lloyd heaved a sigh. "OK, Jamie, but if he does come near you, just let me know," he said.

"His brother's out on bail tomorrow morning. I want to be certain he's keeping his nose clean."

Jamie's heart thumped. Fullwood's brother was out tomorrow. Fullwood's voice rang in Jamie's mind:

"And when my brother gets out on bail, he's goin' to come lookin' for your dad."

Despite everything, Jamie insisted on going to school the next morning. Something inside him felt numb. He just didn't care. Fullwood could punch him or kick him and call him names. Jamie had had his chance to tell PC Lloyd and he'd passed it up. Now whatever happened was his own fault.

Fullwood met him at the gate into school. "My brother's out in a matter of hours and, to celebrate, I'm going to use you as a football after school. Then you can be in the same ward as your dad in hospital."

"Right," Jamie said and walked past him, without even looking back.

At break, Jamie wandered straight up to his old friends. Sam looked around nervously. Faisal stared at the ground. "Look, we're sorry, Jamie…" Isaac started to say.

"Don't worry," Jamie said. "I know I brought this all on myself. If my dad hadn't hit Fullwood's brother and I hadn't gone on about it and tried to be a hero, then everything would've been fine. I'm just sorry I made things worse."

Jamie drifted through the day like a robot, ignoring everything in lessons and everyone at dinner time. Then, just before the bell for home-time, his phone rang. Frowning, he answered.

Mum sobbed on the other end of the line. "Jamie, come home quick," she said. "It's your dad."

CHAPTER 7
HOSPITAL

Jamie stood in silence as he listened to his mum on the phone. "A car," she said. "Hit and run. He's in hospital now. Could be serious."

Without answering, Jamie hurried out of school. Fullwood thundered after him. "Come back here, you fake!" he yelled.

Jamie ignored him until Fullwood overtook him and jumped in front of him. He pushed Jamie back. "Get out of my way, Fullwood," Jamie snapped. "I don't have time for all this."

"Don't have time?" Fullwood shouted, pushing

Jamie. "I'll tell you if you've got time or not."

Quite a crowd had gathered now and Jamie became aware of the audience. "No," he said, calmly, "you won't. Now get out of my way. I'm sick of you making my life a misery. I'm sick of you trying to scare people all the time. What's your problem that you have to pick on little kids like David or someone who can't fight you, like me?"

Fullwood licked his lips and clenched his fists. "Watch your mouth, Garson," he said. "Or..."

"I know what you'll do, you'll hurt me," Jamie said. "Well, if that's all you can do, then get on with it. Go on hit me, if it makes you feel big."

"I'm warning you..." Fullwood started, but he looked uncertain and he kept glancing behind Jamie for some reason.

"My dad didn't go looking for trouble. Your brother chose to rob that shop and we just walked in on him when he was frightening some old man with a baseball bat. He seems a big man, just like you," Jamie said. "So, go on, big man, hit me. Knock me down. Put me in hospital. 'Cos right now, that's where I want to be. With my dad!"

"Go on then, Fullwood," Isaac said, stepping beside Jamie.

"Yeah," Faisal said, joining Isaac, "'Cos if you hurt him, then you're going to have to hurt me too."

"And me," Sam said.

David wriggled out of the crowd. "And me," he said. Jamie swallowed hard and Fullwood lowered his fists as one-by-one, everyone in the crowd stepped forwards beside Jamie. "Just you wait," Fullwood said. "This isn't over…" But Jamie knew it was. Somehow, they'd faced him down and he could see the fight had gone out of Calder Fullwood. With a sneer, Fullwood turned and pushed his way out of the tight circle that had closed around him. Nobody gave an inch and he had to barge some of the bigger students.

"Now run, Jamie," Faisal said, patting him on the back. "Get yourself to your mum and dad!"

And Jamie ran. He ran like he'd never run before.

EPILOGUE

Dad sat up in his hospital bed and munched on a grape. Jamie leaned over and stole a couple from his bag. "Oi, that's thieving, that is," Dad said. "I'll have you for that!"

"Like to see you try old man," Jamie said, grinning at him.

Mum shook her head. "I think we've had enough of stopping robberies, don't you?" she said, raising her eyebrows at Dad.

"Don't worry, I won't be making any citizen's arrests anytime soon," he said, pointing to the big cast on his leg. The doctors said that he was lucky to have got away with a broken leg and a cut on his forehead. "Although, in a way, I caught that Fullwood bloke a second time, didn't I?"

"Yeah, that was really crafty, leaving your blood smeared all over his front bumper, Dad," Jamie said. "Quick thinking too…"

Mum shivered and gave Jamie a nudge. "Don't joke about it like that. It's not funny."

Jamie gave Dad a look and managed to keep his face straight. "So, how's school, now?" Dad asked.

"Fine," Jamie said. "Well, it's still school, but with Calder Fullwood excluded, it's a lot quieter and I've got all my friends back, so, yeah, it's good."

"Great stuff, you see you should've stood up to him from the start," Dad said.

"You should've told someone from the start," Mum said. "Anyway, your dad got picked on all through school, didn't he tell you?"

"Really?" Jamie exclaimed.

"Yeah, by me," Mum said, laughing. "He gave in and married me in the end."

A nurse popped her head around the door. "I'm sorry to disturb you all but there's a news reporter waiting at reception. She wants to know if she can interview you for her paper…"

Dad looked at Mum and then at Jamie. "No," he said. "Could you tell her I'm sick? Sick of newspapers and TV and radio!"

The nurse smiled and went to send the reporter away.

"They'll soon find another hero," he said. "And anyway, I'm not a hero. I'm just an ordinary dad."

Jamie grinned. "Yeah, but you're my ordinary dad!"

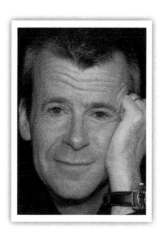

ABOUT THE AUTHOR

Jon Mayhew lives near Liverpool with his family.
He has written many books, including the
award-winning Mortlock horror trilogy and
the Monster Odyssey series. His other titles for
Badger include *Death Road* and *Death Wheels* from
the Teen Reads series.